"Don't worry, master," said the Cat to Jack, for that was the youngest son's name. "I will make you rich."

Jack was surprised to hear that. He was surprised to hear a Cat talk at all. Jack bought his Cat a pair of strong boots, and the Cat went off hunting.

·Favorite Fairy Tales·

Puss In Boots

Retold by Rochelle Larkin   **Illustrated by Loretta Lustig**

Published by Playmore Inc., Publishers, 58 Main Street, 2nd Floor, Hackensack, N.J. 07601
and Waldman Publishing Corp., 570 Seventh Avenue, New York, N.Y. 10018

Conforms to ASTM F963-96a and EN71
Printed in China

Once upon a time, there was a miller who had three sons. When he died, he left his mill to his oldest son, his donkey to his middle son, and to his youngest he left his wonderful Cat.

The Cat caught a big fine rabbit. He popped it right into his bag.

Then off he went to present his catch to the king. The king was well pleased and gave the Cat a rich reward.

On his way back, the Cat met a farmer.

"Whose fields are these?" asked the Cat.

"All this land is owned by a bad ogre," said the farmer, "who keeps us all under his power."

"We'll just see about that," thought the Cat.

The ogre looked very frightening. "What do you want, little one?" he asked.

"I've heard about your magic," said the Cat boldly, "and I don't believe it."

"Why, I can make myself into anything I choose," roared the ogre, "and eat you up as well!"

"Can you make yourself into a lion?" asked the Cat.

"Just like that!" said the ogre, and snapping his fingers, he turned into a roaring lion, mane and tail and all!

The Cat didn't like that very much, but now he knew what to do.
"Can you become a bird?" he asked.
In a flash, the ogre was a giant eagle, flying all over the room.

"It's easy to become bigger than you are," the Cat said. "But can you be as small as a mouse?"

"Watch this!" shouted the ogre. All at once, he was a little gray mouse.

Quickly the cat pounced, and the mouse was gone. No more ogre!

The very next day, the Cat told Jack to swim in the river, while he hid his clothes. Then he ran and stood in the road.

Before long the king came by in his coach.
"Your majesty," said the Cat, taking off his hat and bowing low.
"It's the Cat who brought me the rabbit," said the king to the princess.

"What beautiful green fields," said the princess.

"All this belongs to my master," said the Cat proudly, "as far as the eye can see."

The coach sped along, and everything the king and princess saw, the Cat said belonged to his master.

At last they came to where Jack was swimming in the river.
"Help! Help!" Jack shouted, as the Cat had told him to do.
    "Quick! Stop the coach!" said the Cat. "My master is drowning!"
    "Oh dear!" exclaimed the princess.

The coachman brought a cloak to cover Jack. Shivering, Jack explained that robbers had stolen his clothes as he swam.

"We will take you to the castle and give you proper clothes," said the king. "It's the least we can do for the owner of such fine lands."

When Jack had been dressed in the best clothes at the castle, they all sat down to dinner. The princess thought Jack the handsomest man she had ever seen.

And when Jack explained how the Cat had gotten rid of the terrible ogre, the king's admiration grew. A man who owned so much land, plus a Cat like that, was well worth having for a friend. More than a friend, thought the princess.

When Jack asked the princess to marry him, she said yes.
The king was so happy, he invited Jack's brothers to the castle,
too. They married two ladies of the court.

Jack, his brothers, the whole court, and of course, the Cat lived happily ever after.